No Stone Unturned

by

Brian Keaney

First published in 2001 in Great Britain by
Barrington Stoke Ltd
www.barringtonstoke.co.uk

This edition published 2005

Reprinted 2006

ISBN 1-842993-49-6
13 digit ISBN 978-1-84299-349-1

Printed in Great Britain by Bell & Bain Ltd

A Note from the Author

I wrote this story after I spent a week by myself in an old cottage in Cornwall. There were no electric lights and at night you could hear the waves crashing in the dark.

Do I believe in ghosts? Yes I do. I think they're all around us, just waiting for us to notice them. I think they're the unhappy ones, the people who died full of anger and hate.

You may think I'm talking nonsense. But it's easy to say that when you're sitting at home with the electric light on and your friends or family around you. It's very different when you're on your own in the dark in a wild and lonely place.

Contents

Chapter 1
A Nasty Piece of Work

Everyone round here agrees about David Foster. They shake their heads and say that what happened to him was a terrible thing even though nobody liked him very much when he was alive.

In fact, most people tried their hardest to avoid him. With good reason. He was a nasty piece of work, six feet tall and built like a professional boxer. He had thick, dark hair, even darker eyes and a way of looking at people that made them want to keep their

1

distance. You could tell the first time you met him that it would be a mistake to get on the wrong side of him.

I never had a lot to do with David Foster, but I used to see him when he came into our village pub, *The Ship*. I had a job there, collecting the dirty glasses. I wasn't allowed to serve behind the bar because I was only sixteen at the time, but collecting glasses was OK by me. It was a chance to get to know a bit more about what went on in the village.

I should tell you about the village I live in. It's called Brede and it's a remote place on the Cornish coast. The same families have been living here for generations and they don't take kindly to newcomers, like me.

Yes, I'm a newcomer even though I've grown up here. You see, my family moved here from another village when I was only six, but even after ten years I'm still considered an outsider. That's what they're like in Brede. A close-knit community. So working in the pub was one way for me to get to know people.

Brede is a fishing village. It always has been and always will be. It's pretty enough in the summer months when the tourists come, but cold and bleak in the winter. Then the waves come crashing into the harbour and make the brightly-painted fishing boats bob up and down like corks.

For hundreds of years, the people of Brede have been putting out to sea in those little boats, fishing in the savage waters. It's a dangerous way to earn a living and fishermen don't always come back. Sometimes the sea takes them. That's the way people put it round here. They say the sea is cruel. They talk about it as if it was alive. After you've lived here for a while, you start to think like the locals. You find yourself believing in all sorts of things that people would laugh about anywhere else.

David Foster used to come into *The Ship* every evening at exactly seven thirty. He'd come through the low doorway, bending to avoid the beam over the door. Then he'd shamble up to the bar and bang his money down on the counter.

He never bothered to ask for a drink but Mr Chandler, the landlord, knew what he wanted and poured it out right away. Then he would take his drink to a table in the corner of the pub and sit hunched up over it, not talking to a soul.

Once I made the mistake of trying to take his glass away before he'd finished drinking. He looked up at me and his eyes blazed with fury. I was sure he was going to hit me.

"Sorry," I mumbled as I backed away.

He swore under his breath, then went back to his own dark thoughts. Like I say, he was a nasty piece of work. To tell you the truth, I wasn't that sorry about what

happened to him. It was his wife, Lisa, that I
pitied.

Chapter 2
An Unhappy Woman

Lisa Foster was an unhappy woman. You could tell just by looking at her that she didn't enjoy her life. She went around with a frightened look on her face and she never looked anyone in the eyes.

If you spoke to her, she looked down at the ground and spoke very quietly in reply. Everyone knew the reason why. Her husband was a jealous man and it was said that he could be violent. Nobody wanted to find out whether or not the gossip was true, so very few people ever spoke to Lisa Foster unless they had to.

Lisa and David Foster had terrible rows. I know that because my girlfriend, Emma, lived right next door to them. She used to tell me that she would hear David Foster shouting at his wife. Sometimes there would be the crash of something being thrown across the room. Then he would slam the door behind him and march off to the pub. Afterwards Lisa Foster could be heard sobbing by herself in the empty house.

Maybe someone should have done something about it earlier, called the police, perhaps. But there was no real evidence and Lisa Foster certainly never complained. She just carried on in the same unhappy way. Of course, she never came into the village pub with her husband. But Emma told me that she sometimes saw her walking along the cliffs beyond the village with their dog, a labrador named Petra.

The cliffs beyond the village of Brede are well-known for being wild, rugged and dangerous but they are also very beautiful. If you follow the little path out of the village you soon find yourself on a narrow track that leads over the sand hills to the cliff-top. You can stand there on those dunes and look out at the ever-changing sea, or listen to the roar of the waves as they come rolling in and break into white foam against the black rocks below.

Most of the villagers stay away from the cliff-top paths. They have enough of the sea every day of their lives. They don't have to go out for a walk to admire it. But I sometimes go that way with Emma. I like looking at the rocks. If I was an artist I would paint them. There are rocks like huge great fingers that stick out of the water some way out to sea and there are great slabs of rock closer to the shore that look as if they are the remains of some ancient building.

At the base of the cliffs, the rocks are piled up in heaps where the sea has dumped them, like toys left behind by some giant child. Sometimes if you look down for too long you can feel the urge to throw yourself onto them. You wonder what it would be like to step over the cliff into nothingness. What would you think about as you fell? What would go through your mind in that moment before you hit the ground?

That's when it's time to turn round and head back for the bright lights of the village.

Th.

Chapter 3
The Townie

If there's one sort of person the people of Brede dislike it's a townie – someone who comes from the town or city. They say that townies don't understand our ways and perhaps they're right.

Simon Scrivener certainly didn't understand the village of Brede and perhaps the village of Brede didn't understand him either.

Of course everyone knew who he was before he even moved into the big house on the outskirts of the village. That house used to belong to old Doctor Harris, but it had been empty since his death a year ago. It caused quite a stir in the bar of *The Ship* when someone said that it had been bought by a townie. And it wasn't long before everyone knew the townie's name.

Simon Scrivener was a famous writer of detective stories. His books had been made into films and he had been interviewed on the television more than once. But that didn't impress the people of Brede. As far as they were concerned he was just another townie who didn't understand the ways of the village. They were determined to dislike him from the start.

I liked Simon, but maybe that's just because we were both outsiders. He was certainly generous enough with his money. He would buy a drink for anyone who walked into *The Ship* and try to get chatting with them. Most people were polite, though not exactly friendly. David Foster, of course, couldn't even manage to be polite.

I remember when it happened.

Simon Scrivener was standing at the bar. He was a tall man in his thirties, good-looking with sandy hair that fell over his forehead. He had a habit of brushing it back with his hand every now and then. You could tell that he had money. It wasn't the way he dressed, it was more the way he behaved. He had such confidence. That evening, he had been talking to the landlord about the cliffs, when David Foster came into the bar. Simon turned towards him at once and held out his hand, smiling, "I'm Simon Scrivener," he said, "I've just moved into the village." David Foster walked past him without a glance and went over to the bar.

Simon was not put off that easily. He withdrew his hand but kept on smiling. "Let me buy you a drink," he said.

This time David Foster spoke. "I don't want your drink," he said, looking straight ahead of him. "And I don't want to talk to you either." Then he slammed his money down on the bar as he always did.

Simon shrugged it off but his lips formed a thin line of anger. It was the only time that he and David Foster ever spoke to each other. That was surprising when you consider everything that happened afterwards.

Chapter 4
A Twist of Fate

In every story there is always a turning point when Fate takes over. Sometimes it's hard to work out exactly when that happens. At other times it's very clear. In this case it seems to me that Fate stepped in when Simon Scrivener and Lisa Foster both decided to go walking along the same cliff-top path on the same evening. Lisa was walking her dog. Simon was simply admiring the view. Lisa let Petra off the lead as she always did and the dog ran off at once and vanished over the sand dunes. When Lisa caught up with Petra, she found that Simon was already making friends with the dog. He had been standing on the path watching the evening sun turning the sky and the sea a dozen different shades of gold when the dog had come sniffing up to him.

That was how Simon and Lisa came to speak to each other. Simon told me about it later on when I got to know him a little better. By the time Lisa came up, Petra was licking his hand in a friendly way and refused to come away when she was called. I expect Simon was the one who spoke first. He probably stuck out his hand and introduced himself exactly as he had done to her husband.

Of course Lisa knew who he was already. She had heard the local gossip just like everyone else. Perhaps her husband had told her about the new owner of Dr Harris' old house, a man who thought he could win friends simply by buying them a drink. That was how David Foster would have seen it, of course. But Lisa looked at things in a different way. Though she wasn't used to people being friendly towards her, she liked it when they were, all the more so when the person being friendly was both famous and good-looking.

I don't know exactly what Simon and Lisa said to each other, but I can just see him pushing back the hair that fell over his forehead and talking about how beautiful the light was on the sea.

I expect she asked him how he was settling in. Maybe she even dared to ask him about his books. I am sure he would have asked Lisa about herself and she would have told him that she worked in the local supermarket and lived in one of the little cottages near the harbour. At the time, she probably felt ashamed as she told him all this.

After all, he was rich and famous. Why on earth would he be interested to hear about her everyday life?

But he *was* interested. Very interested. The very first moment he saw her coming along the path looking for Petra, Simon was interested. He told us that. He told Emma and me everything. That was only natural. After all, we were involved.

Chapter 5
No Turning Back

That meeting was the first of many. Soon
it was clear to anyone who saw Lisa Foster
going about the village that a big change had
taken place in her life. She no longer went
about looking like a frightened rabbit.
Instead she had a secret smile on her face
and she stared into the distance as if she was
looking into a future that was bright and
rosy.

If anyone in the village had bothered to look, they would have seen that Simon Scrivener had the same look about him. He was a happy man. Until then, success had not brought him what he was looking for. That was one reason why he had moved from London. He had been tired of life in the fast lane. He had been looking for a simpler way of life and for someone he could open his heart to. Lisa Foster was that person. She was perfect. There was just one problem: David Foster.

Simon and Lisa talked about David, of course. In fact sometimes it seemed that he was their only topic of conversation.

"He's the most selfish man in the world," Lisa told Simon, "and he's terribly jealous. If he finds out I've been meeting you, I don't know what he'll do." She shuddered when she said this and there was real fear in her eyes.

Simon put his arm around her. "I won't let him do anything to you," he said. It was the first time he had touched her and he was waiting for her to push his hand away but she did not.

All the same, she shook her head sadly. "He could kill you," she said. "He wouldn't care. David's capable of anything."

"I can't understand why you don't want to leave him," Simon said.

Lisa moved away from Simon then and stood looking out to sea. She was so close to the cliff-face that for a moment Simon was terrified she would go tumbling over the edge. Then she turned back and stepped away from the edge and he relaxed again. "I was brought up to believe that marriage is forever," she said bitterly.

Simon shook his head. "Nothing is forever," he said. Then he kissed her and from that moment onwards they both knew there was no turning back.

Chapter 6
Breaking the News

You can't keep something secret for very long in a place like Brede. Both Simon and Lisa knew it was only a matter of time before David Foster found out what was going on. They had to act soon before things came to a head by themselves.

Simon wanted to go with Lisa to the little cottage near the harbour and confront her husband with the truth. But she shook her head. "If you come with me, it will only make things worse," she said, "this is something I've got to do on my own."

Simon wasn't happy at the idea of Lisa facing David Foster by herself. He had seen enough of her husband in the bar of *The Ship* to know that he was a strong man and that he had an ugly temper, but Lisa had made her mind up.

It was a Friday night when Lisa decided to tell David. She and Simon had been walking along the cliff-top path hand in hand. The sea that evening was strangely calm. Its surface was gently rippling and it seemed to Simon like the skin of some huge animal. Lisa suddenly stopped, let go of Simon's hand and said, "I'm going to tell him now."

A chill went through Simon when she said these words and he tried to persuade her to wait just a few more days. "Maybe we could just vanish together without anyone knowing," he suggested.

"I'm not running away," Lisa said. "I've been afraid of him for too long. Meeting you has given me courage."

"What will you say?" Simon asked in a worried voice.

"I'll just tell him that it's over between us, that I've met someone else and that I'm leaving him."

"What do you think he'll do?" asked Simon.

"I don't know. But whatever it is my life can't be any worse than it has been up till now."

But she was wrong about that and afterwards Simon was to remember those words bitterly. Her life could be much, much worse than it had been before. The trouble was that they were both so much in love that they were blind. They didn't see just how much evil was hidden in David Foster's soul.

"Wait here," Lisa said. "I'll come back to you when I've told him the news."

"What about all your things at the cottage?" Simon asked her. "You can't just leave them there."

She shook her head. "There's nothing in that cottage that I want," she said, "I'm going to leave my old life behind and start again." Then she walked away from Simon.

As he stood and watched her go, he wondered if he would ever see her again.

Simon watched the gulls as they wheeled overhead. Their harsh cries were sad and lonely, just as his own life had been until he had met Lisa. Again and again, he wished he had insisted on going with her to the cottage. Maybe it was not too late. Maybe he should follow her now, knock on the door of the cottage and speak to David Foster himself. Just as he was about to move off, he saw her walking towards him along the cliff-top path.

She was smiling all over her face. "What happened?" he asked as he ran to meet her.

"I told him," she said.

"And what did he say?"

She shrugged. "He called me all sorts of names but he didn't try to stop me. I think he must have known that there was nothing that he could do."

"Did he threaten you?" Simon asked.

"Not really. He just said I'd regret what I'd done and I told him he was wrong. Then I turned round and walked out."

"Is that all?" Simon asked. "It couldn't have been *that* simple."

"Yes, it was."

"I can't believe it."

"Well, it's true," Lisa said.

"Wasn't he even angry?" Simon asked her.

"I suppose he must have been," she said, "but do you know what?"

"What?"

"As I walked out the door he was smiling."

"Smiling?"

"Yes. It wasn't a nice smile, of course. It was a horrible smile, as if he knew something that I didn't." She shuddered. "Anyway I did it. I told him." As she said these words she began to weep from pure relief.

Simon put his arms around her and hugged her. "It's all right," he said, "you can come home with me now. The nightmare's over."

But he was wrong. The nightmare was only just beginning.

Chapter 7
A Knock at the Door

The next morning there was a loud knocking at the door of the house which had once belonged to old Doctor Harris. Simon Scrivener came downstairs in his dressing-gown, brushing the hair from his forehead as he opened the door. A policeman and a policewoman were standing on the doorstep. They asked to speak to Lisa Foster.

"What do you want her for?" Simon demanded but they wouldn't tell him.

Lisa herself came to the door just then. "I'm Lisa Foster," she told them. "What is it?"

"I'm afraid we've got some bad news for you, Mrs Foster," the policewoman said. "Perhaps we'd better come inside."

They all went into the kitchen and sat down. The policewoman looked at the policeman nervously and then she began to explain how David Foster's body had been found at the bottom of the cliffs in the early hours of the morning.

"Did he fall?" Lisa asked in a shocked voice.

"That's what we thought at first," the policeman said. "Then we discovered this in one of his pockets." He handed a letter to Lisa. She took it out of the envelope and read it slowly. She didn't say a word but all the colour drained out of her face. Then she handed it to Simon.

The letter made it clear that David Foster *had* meant to kill himself. His words were full of anger and bitterness. He blamed his wife for what had happened and he refused to accept that she had been free to leave him. At the very end he had written, *You will always be my wife. You will never be free of me.*

"Who found him?" Lisa asked. She sounded stunned.

"One of the neighbours saw the dog standing at the edge of the cliff and barking madly," the policeman told her.

"Petra?"

"I don't know the name, I'm afraid, madam. It was a labrador."

"She was *our* dog," Lisa said. "I should never have left her behind."

"The people next door are taking care of her for the present," the policeman said.

The police asked Lisa to come with them to identify the body formally. "But you already know who it is!" Simon said, angrily.

"It's just routine, sir," the policeman told him. "It has to be someone who knows the person well."

"It's all right, Simon," Lisa said. "I don't mind."

"I'm afraid you'll find it very distressing. The injuries to the body were terrible. He fell a long way," the policewoman said. She spoke as gently as she could.

Lisa nodded. "I understand," she said. She stood up. "I'm ready," she told them. Then she went out of the house and got in the police car.

Chapter 8
The Dream

The police were as kind as they could be, but of course they had questions to ask and the whole thing took its toll on Lisa. She looked pale and worn out.

The story of what had happened soon spread right through the village. "What could you expect from a townie?" the villagers asked. But they didn't really blame Simon. As far as they were concerned, it was Lisa who was to blame. She had been brought up in Brede but she had turned her back on the village. They shook their heads in disgust and once again she looked down at the ground as she went about her business, frightened to look anyone in the eye.

Not everyone felt the same way. My girlfriend Emma's family was kind to Lisa. It was her father who found the body and they ended up looking after Petra until Lisa came and asked for her back. "You should have seen her," Emma told me afterwards. "She looked as if she didn't know what she was doing, as if she was in a daze."

Emma felt sorry for her and offered to take Petra out for walks when she needed exercise. Lisa Foster was happy to accept. She needed all the help she could get.

It was the night after the funeral that Lisa had the dream. Simon was woken up by an ear-splitting scream. Terrified, he switched on the bedside light. Lisa was sitting up in bed staring in front of her. Her eyes were wide with terror.

"What is it?" he asked her.

With a shaking hand she pointed. "He was there," she said. "Just a moment ago."

"Who was?"

"David. He was standing there looking at me and he was covered in blood. He was holding something in his hand. I couldn't see what it was but he was beckoning me to come closer. He wanted me to come and look at what he was holding."

"It was a dream," Simon told her. He put his arm around her but she shook it off.

"It wasn't a dream," she said. "I saw him. And he was smiling. The same smile he had on his face the night I left him." She shuddered at the memory.

"Of course you thought you saw him,"

Simon told her gently. "It's not surprising after what you've been through, but believe me, Lisa, it was a nightmare. Now why don't you lie down and go to sleep?"

But she wouldn't listen to him. "David was standing right there by the window," she said, "and he was holding something in his hand but what was it?" She stared at Simon as if *he* might know the answer to her question.

He put his arm round her. "You've been through a terrible time lately," he said. "It's understandable."

She shook off his arm. "Why won't you listen to me?" she said.

"It's all over now, Lisa," he said, trying to sound as soothing as he could. "Just forget about it and go back to sleep."

She gave him a look then that he would never forget, as if she thought he was crazy. "Of course it's not over," she said. "It'll never be over."

Chapter 9
Nerves

As time went on, Lisa showed no sign of getting over the terrible experience that she had been through. If anything, she grew worse. She gave up her job in the supermarket and sat about the house moping.

Sometimes Simon would find her standing in the middle of the room holding a cup or a broom and just gazing blankly in front of her. It was as if she had forgotten what she was doing a moment before. She seemed to be

having trouble remembering all sorts of
things. Sometimes she would arrange for
Emma to come and walk Petra in the
afternoon. But when Emma turned up, Lisa
had forgotten all about the plan and would
simply stare at Emma as if she could not
recall who she was.

One evening, Lisa told Simon that she
wanted to go out for a walk by herself. He at
once offered to come with her, but she said
that she wanted to be alone. He tried to
convince her that this was not a good idea,
but she insisted. So he waited until she had
left, then he went out the door and secretly
followed her.

Lisa took the lonely path across the sand
dunes to the cliffs. She never once looked
behind her. Simon knew where she was going
of course. She was making straight for the
spot where David Foster had thrown himself
onto the rocks.

When she got there, she stood looking down and Simon waited, too terrified to make a sound, in case he startled her and she tumbled to her death. Then, when he thought he could bear it no longer, she turned back and walked past him as though she hadn't seen him.

Simon began to be afraid to leave Lisa alone for any length of time. She was starting to do the oddest things. One day he found her in the kitchen holding the electric kettle and staring at it. "It's broken," she told him. He looked at it. The base was burnt and the plastic feet on which it stood had all melted. He glanced at the gas cooker. Black plastic had melted around one ring.

"Did you put this on the gas?" he asked her.

"Of course not," Lisa said but it was quite clear that she was lying.

Another morning he woke up to find her making breakfast. She was boiling a saucepan full of milk and cornflakes. The whole thing was a soggy mess. He took the pan from her and looked inside. The cornflakes were all stuck to the bottom of the pan.

Later that day he telephoned the doctor who agreed to come to the house and see her. "I don't know what you want to call *him* for," Lisa said. "There's nothing the matter with me." She sounded cross, as if she thought he was making a fuss about nothing.

There was no need to explain to the doctor what Lisa Foster had been through. He knew everyone in the village. He was quite a nervous man, bald, with thick glasses. He hesitated when he spoke as if he was never sure what he was going to say. He asked Lisa whether she was having problems sleeping at night. She shook her head.

"She had a terrible nightmare a short time ago," Simon told him.

"It wasn't a nightmare," she said sharply.

"And she sometimes forgets things," he went on.

"I don't forget the things that matter," she said.

The doctor looked from one to the other, as if he was not sure who he should be listening to. Then he took out his prescription pad. "Probably suffering from nerves," he said. "This should help." He wrote out a prescription for some tablets, then hurried out of the house.

The tablets did not help. Simon was not even sure that she took them. He went to the chemist himself with the prescription, brought the tablets back and explained carefully how many she was to take each day.

But he had a strong feeling that she was not listening to a word he said.

It was a few days after the doctor called that Lisa began to look for her wedding ring. That was when things got really bad.

Chapter 10
Looking for the Ring

It began in the middle of the night. Simon woke up to find Lisa out of bed, searching in the drawer of the dressing table. At first, he thought she must have been having another nightmare. He rubbed his eyes. "What's the matter?" he asked sleepily.

She didn't answer him. Instead she carried on with her search.

"What are you looking for?" he asked her again, sitting up in bed. He was wide awake now and he could see that the other drawers of the dressing table had been pulled open and everything tipped out on the floor.

Lisa turned towards him and there was a wild look in her eyes. "My ring," she said, "my wedding ring. Where is it?"

Simon looked at her in surprise. "I don't know," he said. He could remember her taking it off the evening she had left David. As they had walked hand in hand back to his house she had slipped the ring from her finger and put it in her pocket, but he had not seen it since that day. "You must have put it away somewhere," he said. "We'll look for it in the morning."

"You've hidden it!" she said, her eyes blazing.

"Don't be so silly!" he said. "Why would I do that?"

Lisa ignored the question. "I'm going to find it even if it takes all night," she said. She turned back to the drawer and continued her frantic search.

Simon sighed. He got out of bed and went over to her. He put his hand on her arm. "You're just getting yourself all worked up," he said but she pushed him away angrily.

"Don't lie to me!" she said.

Simon was shocked. "I'm not lying!" he said. How could she accuse him of that? He would never lie to her. Surely she must know that? What was happening to her? He couldn't understand. It seemed as if she was losing her mind.

"Please come back to bed," he said but Lisa took no notice. Instead she went out of the bedroom and began searching in the living room downstairs.

He thought about going after her but he was very tired and she was not in a mood to be reasonable. He decided that there was nothing more he could do for now. So he went back to bed and lay there for a long time, listening to the sound of Lisa emptying out every drawer and every cupboard in the house.

It was morning before he fell asleep and Lisa had still not stopped searching.

Chapter 11
Noises in the Night

From then on, Lisa never stopped looking for the ring. It became an obsession with her. She searched the house over and over again. Then she began wandering into the village, stopping people in the street and asking them if they had seen it. She even asked complete strangers.

Soon people began to avoid her. When they saw her coming, they would cross over to the other side of the road. Of course

Simon tried to stop her doing this but it was hopeless. She would not listen to a word he said. He was at his wit's end. He did not know what to do or how to cope. In the end, he called out the doctor again, who prescribed stronger tablets for Lisa. But these were no more use than the last lot. The strain was beginning to tell on Simon. He felt he couldn't cope much longer. Then came the noises in the night.

It happened on the one night when Lisa had fallen into a deep sleep. She had spent the entire day searching in the garden for her ring. It was after dark when she came indoors, lay down on the bed fully-dressed and fell asleep. Simon knew that he should take this chance to get some sleep himself, but he could not rest. He lay in bed listening to the old grandfather clock striking the hours.

The clock had just struck midnight when there was a noise downstairs. Simon sat up in bed. What was that? He listened carefully. There was no sound. Had he imagined it? No! There it was again. It sounded like somebody moving about downstairs. He turned on the bedside light. Lisa was lying next to him sound asleep. Then who could it be?

He got out of bed very quietly, put on his dressing gown and a pair of slippers, then looked around for some sort of weapon. There was a brass candlestick on the dressing table and he grabbed this. Then he crept out of the room and slowly went down the stairs.

Simon could hear the noise more closely now. It sounded like someone walking backwards and forwards across the room. He was not easily scared. He was a strong man and he knew how to look after himself. But as he got closer, he felt more frightened than he had ever been before. There was something going on that did not feel right. He felt as if he, himself, were being watched, as if the whole house was somehow awake and listening.

That was a stupid thought, he told himself and he tried to put it out of his mind as he reached the bottom of the stairs. He paused before opening the door to the living room. Suddenly there was a crash of broken glass. With his heart beating madly, he flung open the door and switched on the light.

On the floor near the table was a broken wine glass, but the room was empty. There was an unpleasant smell in there, a smell of damp and decay that made him feel sick. He looked around the room but there was nowhere that a person could hide. Getting more and more nervous, he went into each of the other downstairs rooms. There was no-one there.

When he was sure that there was nobody in the house, Simon opened the back door and stepped outside. Still holding the brass candlestick he looked all around. It was a cloudless night and the sky was full of stars. At any other time he would have stopped to admire the night sky. But not tonight. He went to look at Petra's kennel. If there had been anybody there, he told himself, Petra would have barked.

He found the dog shivering in the back of her kennel. Her eyes were wild and her fur was standing up on end. She whimpered when she saw him. He put down the candlestick and stroked her gently. "It's all right, Petra," he told her. "It's all right, old girl."

Suddenly the dog seemed to catch sight of something behind Simon and let out a chilling howl. Simon spun round. As he did, he thought he saw a shape disappearing round the side of the house. Fear ran through his body like icy water. He seized the candlestick again and ran in the direction the shape had taken. But when he got there he saw nothing and no-one. Taking great care, he went all the way round the house, but there was nobody.

Maybe there had been no shape, he told himself. Maybe his nerves had just been unsettled by the dog howling. Maybe his mind was playing tricks on him. But what about the broken wine glass? He couldn't think of a simple explanation for it, though he could easily guess what Lisa would have said. She would have said it was David Foster. Well he wasn't going to believe in stuff like that. He went back inside, taking care to lock the door carefully behind him. He found a dustpan and brush and swept up the broken glass. Then he went back upstairs to bed where Lisa was just as he had left her. He got into bed beside her and lay down, but there would be no more sleep for him that night.

Chapter 12

In the Gutter

A few days later things came to a head. Simon had fallen asleep in the middle of the afternoon. He was so tired these days that sometimes he could not help himself dropping off. When he woke up he saw at once that Lisa was gone. He ran through the house looking for her. Then he grabbed his coat and headed for the cliff-top paths. That was his greatest fear – that one day she would fall off the edge of the cliff while searching for her ring.

Simon took Petra with him, hoping the dog might find Lisa even if *he* could not. Together they raced across the sand dunes towards the cliffs. But when they got there they could find no sign of her.

Terrified, Simon made his way to the spot where David Foster had jumped to his death. He stood on the edge of the cliff and forced himself to look down at the deadly rocks below. He dreaded what he might see there. But there was no sign of Lisa.

Relieved, he turned back and continued along the path past his own house and into the village itself. And that was where he found her. To his horror, he saw that she was down on her hands and knees outside the post office searching in the gutter for her ring. People were standing in the street looking at her. Some of them were laughing, others were shaking their heads in pity, but Lisa was taking no notice of them.

Simon quickly went over to Lisa, took her arm and brought her to her feet. She did not want to give up her search but in the end she allowed him to lead her home.

All the time she continued to talk about her wedding ring. Where could it possibly be? Had he put it somewhere? Simon had heard these questions so often that he had given up trying to answer them. He walked beside her in silence, wondering what he should do next. He knew that things had gone too far. When they got home he telephoned for the doctor again.

This time the doctor spread his hands wide. "I've done all I can," he said. "I'm afraid she needs to see a specialist. I'll make an appointment at the local hospital."

A few days later, Simon drove Lisa to the hospital. Even there he had difficulty keeping her from thinking about her ring. She kept wanting to open doors and search rooms marked STAFF ONLY. As they sat in the waiting room outside the clinic door, she spent the whole time talking to the other patients, asking them whether they had seen her ring.

At last it was her turn to be seen. Simon went into the consulting room with her. The consultant was a middle-aged woman with short, grey hair and a habit of peering over her glasses at people. She listened carefully to everything that Simon told her, nodding her head and making notes. Then she said she would like to talk to Lisa by herself. So Simon went outside and waited. He grew more and more anxious. At last the door opened and the consultant came out. There was a frown on her face. "I'm afraid Lisa is a very sick woman," she said. "I think it's best if we keep her here in hospital for the time being."

"But have you found out what's wrong with her?" Simon asked.

The consultant shook her head. "This is a complex case. We'll have to observe and carry out a few tests. Don't worry. She's in the best place now. We'll look after her. I suggest you go home and get some rest, Mr Scrivener. You look quite worn out."

Chapter 13

On the Cliff-top

It was true, Simon was quite worn out. When he got back that evening, he went indoors and sat down, feeling he never wanted to get up again. The last few months had been a terrible strain. It was a great relief to know that somebody else was now responsible for looking after Lisa. He felt sure that the doctors at the hospital would be able to cure her. All he had to do now was to wait for her to come home.

Then Simon heard Petra whining. He had forgotten about her. She had been tied up all day. He felt too tired and upset to take the dog out himself. So he phoned Emma and asked her if she would take the dog out. Emma agreed, even though it was late. She phoned me up and asked to see if I would come along too.

That's how I came to be there and that's how I know that this story is true. I saw it all happen with my own eyes.

It was already dark when Emma and I got to Simon's house. As he opened the door to us he looked like a different man to the successful writer who had arrived from London only a few months ago. His face was lined with worry. I wouldn't have changed places with him then for all the money in the world. We went round to Petra's kennel at the back of the house. She was glad to see us. She leaped up on me licking my face. I held her while Emma attached the lead and then we set off across the sand dunes.

If you've never lived right out in the country, then you probably don't know how dark it gets at nightfall. When I say dark, I mean really dark. Not like in the towns and cities where there are always streetlamps or lights in shops and houses. Out here it gets pitch-black as soon as you leave the outskirts of Brede. There are no lights to guide you across the sand dunes or along the narrow cliff-top paths. To tell you the truth, it's a dangerous place to be after dark, unless you know your way. But I've walked every inch of those paths and I know them like the back of my hand. So I wasn't worried about the dark that night. But I have to admit that as we walked along the narrow path, I felt nervous. They say that each of us has five senses but there are some people who have one more, a sixth sense. Maybe that was what I felt as I walked along, holding onto Petra's lead. Emma was coming along behind me, but we couldn't walk side by side because there wasn't enough room on the path.

It was a cloudy night and when the moon went behind the clouds you could hardly see more than a metre in front of you. That's what it was like when we drew near the spot where David Foster had jumped to his death. Petra had been running on ahead but suddenly she stopped and started sniffing at something on the ground. Just at that moment, the moon came out from behind the clouds and I saw that there was something bright glinting on the path ahead of me. I stopped.

"What is it?" Emma asked.

"I don't know," I said. I bent down to look more closely, but as I was about to pick it up I became aware that someone was standing in front of me, someone who had not been there a moment ago. Even though the figure before me was standing in the shadows I knew perfectly well who it was. I started to shake all over as a hand covered in blood reached down and picked up the glittering object. David Foster was standing there on the path ahead of me and as he bent forward, the moon lit up his smashed and bloody face.

I wanted to turn and run but I couldn't move. I felt as if all the air was being pressed out of my chest. I was aware of Emma standing behind me and I knew that she, too, was rooted to the spot. As we watched he held up the thing that had been lying on the ground so that the moonlight fell clearly upon it. I could see now that it was a plain gold wedding ring. Then he spoke. "She'll never rest until she finds it," he said. "But she'll never find it." With one movement he swung his arm and flung the ring out over the cliff-edge and into the sea.

"Tell Simon what I did," he went on. He stared right into my eyes as he spoke and I will never, ever, forget that look. It was a glimpse of pure evil. I think if I could have thrown myself off the cliff right then I would have done so, just to get away from that look.

The creature that had once been David Foster smiled, a cold, cruel smile and he spoke again. "Tell him he was wrong," he said. "He couldn't take Lisa from me. You see some things are forever." Then just as suddenly as he had appeared, he was gone.

****

That's more or less the end of my story. I'm afraid that Lisa Foster never did come home, but she's well looked after. Simon goes to visit her, but he's not sure she even knows who he is anymore. She only ever talks about one thing, the wedding ring she lost. It looks as if David Foster was right. She'll never stop looking for it as long as she lives.

Barrington Stoke would like to thank all its readers for commenting on the manuscript before publication and in particular:

Sandra Agombar	Marcus Guest
Maxwell Amies	Marcelina Hamilton
Victoria Bellingham	Natasha Hamilton
William Blackham	Nick Jordan
Chris Brooks	Christopher Heywood
Adam Buckland	Ben King-Warner
Josh Chandler	Tom Metcalfe
James Clark	Jill Nowland
Richard Barrie Clay	Karl Oreyer
Cherise Cross	Alex Patterson
Vivian Faichney	James Pearce
George Field	Sam Randolph
Kenny Field	Hilary Riches
Nikki Fine	John Simpson
	James A. Turner

Become a Consultant!

Would you like to give us feedback on our titles before they are published? Contact us at the email address below – we'd love to hear from you!

E-mail: info@barringtonstoke.co.uk
Website: www.barringtonstoke.co.uk

Hard-hitting short reads from Barrington Stoke

RIME

Prisoner in Alcatraz	Theresa Breslin	1-84299-150-7 / 978-1-84299-150-3
Bloodline	Kevin Brooks	1-84299-202-3 / 978-1-84299-202-9
Twocking	Eric Brown	1-84299-042-X / 978-1-84299-042-1
Old Bag	Melvin Burgess	1-84299-422-0 / 978-1-84299-422-1
Partners in Crime	Nigel Hinton	1-84299-102-7 / 978-1-84299-102-2
Snapshot	Robert Swindells	1-84299-347-X / 978-1-84299-347-7

DRAMA

I See You Baby	Kevin Brooks & Catherine Forde	1-84299-330-5 / 978-184299-330-9
Baby Baby	Viv French	1-84299-061-6 / 978-1-84299-061-2
Falling Awake	Viv French	1-84299-438-7 / 978-1-84299-4
The Wedding Present	Adèle Geras	1-84299-348-8 / 978-1-84299-348-4
No Stone Unturned	Brian Keaney	1-84299-349-6 / 978-1-84299-349-1
Stalker	Anthony Masters	1-84299-081-0 / 978-1-84299-081-0
The Blessed and the Damned	Sara Sheridan	1-84299-008-X / 978-1-84299-008-7

HORROR/SF

Before Night Falls	Keith Gray	1-84299-124-8 / 978-1-84299-124-4
The Dogs	Mark Morris	1-902260-76-7 / 978-1-902260-76-1
House of Lazarus	James Lovegrove	1-84299-125-6 / 978-1-84299-125-1

Other titles by Barrington Stoke ...

Old Bag

by Melvin Burgess

ISBN 1-84299-422-0
13 digit ISBN 9-78-1-84299-422-1

In gangland, you play by the rules if you know what's good for you. And Mikey knows all the rules.

- Don't talk to the filth
- Don't fall in love with the wrong girl, or the girl from the wrong family
- And don't *ever* cross Mrs Crabs

Mikey knows the rules, all right. It's just a pity he's too stupid to stick to them ...

You can order *Old Bag* directly from our website at
www.barringtonstoke.co.uk

Other titles by Barrington Stoke ...

Stalker

by Anthony Masters

ISBN 1-84299-081-0
13 digit ISBN 978-1-84299-081-0

An unseen presence creeping up behind you. Threats of violence behind closed doors. Sarah inhabits an uncertain world where it seems no-one can be trusted – least of all the people who say they care. Running away is not the answer. It only leads to fresh terror with no clear means of escape.

Will the final outcome be a happy one?

You can order *Stalker* directly from our website at **www.barringtonstoke.co.uk**